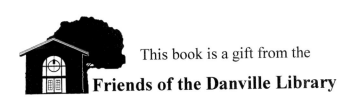

OPERATION: HUTTLET

Adapted by Steele Tyler Filipek

Based on the movie STAR WARS: THE CLONE WARS

WITHDRAWN

Grosset & Dunlap · LucasBooks

GROSSET & DUNLAP
Published by the Penguin Group
Penguin Group (USA) Inc., 375 Hudson Street, New York, New York 10014, USA
Penguin Group (Canada), 90 Eglinton Avenue East, Suite 700,
Toronto, Ontario M4P 2Y3, Canada
(a division of Pearson Penguin Canada Inc.)
Penguin Books Ltd., 80 Strand, London WC2R 0RL, England
Penguin Group Ireland, 25 St. Stephen's Green, Dublin 2, Ireland
(a division of Penguin Books Ltd.)
Penguin Group (Australia), 250 Camberwell Road,
Camberwell, Victoria 3124, Australia
(a division of Pearson Australia Group Pty. Ltd.)
Penguin Books India Pvt. Ltd., 11 Community Centre,
Panchsheel Park, New Delhi—110 017, India
Penguin Group (NZ), 67 Apollo Drive, Rosedale, North Shore 0632, New Zealand
(a division of Pearson New Zealand Ltd.)
Penguin Books (South Africa) (Pty.) Ltd., 24 Sturdee Avenue,
Rosebank, Johannesburg 2196, South Africa

Penguin Books Ltd., Registered Offices:
80 Strand, London WC2R 0RL, England

This book is published in partnership with LucasBooks, a division of Lucasfilm Ltd.

The publisher does not have any control over and does not assume any responsibility
for author or third-party websites or their content.

The scanning, uploading, and distribution of this book via the Internet or via any
other means without the permission of the publisher is illegal and punishable by law.
Please purchase only authorized electronic editions and do not participate in or
encourage electronic piracy of copyrighted materials. Your support of the
author's rights is appreciated.

Library of Congress Cataloging-in-Publication Data is available.

ISBN: 978-0-448-44995-1   10 9 8 7 6 5 4 3 2 1

GLOSSARY

Here are some *Clone Wars* terms that might help you along the way.

Blaster: The main weapon used in the galaxy.

Clone troopers: Identical soldiers bred and trained to serve in the Galactic Republic's army.

Droid: A robot or android.

Energy shield: A protective barrier made of energy.

The Force: An energy field created by all living things. It gives the Jedi their power.

Galactic Republic: The government that rules the galaxy.

Hologram: A projected image of a person.

Hutts: Huge, slug-like creatures. They control many planets on the edge of the galaxy.

Jedi: Masters of the Force. They use their power to protect the Republic.

Lightsaber: The weapon of a Jedi. It looks like a sword made of colored energy.

Padawan: A young Jedi in training.

Separatist Alliance: The group trying to take over the Galactic Republic.

Tatooine: A desert planet. It is hot, far away, and also the home of Jabba the Hutt.

Vulture droids: Large ships that can turn into walking droids.

Youngling: A child who might one day become a Jedi.

CHAPTER 1

The first time Ahsoka Tano and Anakin Skywalker met, they weren't too sure that they would get along. Anakin was a famous Jedi, after all, and Ahsoka was just a young Padawan. He didn't want a little girl tagging along on his dangerous missions. And she didn't like that he treated her like a child. But Master Yoda had assigned Ahsoka to be Anakin's Padawan and to assist him on planet Christophsis. Master Yoda was the wisest of all the Jedi and no one questioned his decisions.

When Ahsoka first arrived, Anakin was too busy for her. He thought she was just a kid and would only get in the way. *I'm not just a kid*, Ahsoka fumed. *I'm a Jedi!*

This was during the Clone Wars. Count Dooku, a former Jedi, had started a war and a lot of planets had joined with him. They were called the Separatist Alliance, and the Republic had to stop them.

The planet Christophsis was under attack and Jedi Master Obi-Wan Kenobi was leading the Republic's clone army into battle against the Separatists' droid army.

It looked bad at first. The Separatists had
a gigantic energy shield and the clone troopers
couldn't pass through it. But luckily, Anakin had
a plan.

Ahsoka and Anakin snuck behind enemy lines,
and Anakin jumped out and started attacking
the droids. That was just a distraction, though. It
was Ahsoka's job to set explosive charges around
the shield generator. But when she finished she
noticed that Anakin was surrounded by enemy
droids. Ahsoka had to help, so she used the Force
to pull a wall down on top of the droids. It was a

close call; the wall crashed down around Anakin, just missing him on all sides. Although he was safe, Anakin was *very* angry at Ahsoka.

"You could have gotten me killed!" Anakin yelled. Ahsoka frowned; she hadn't really thought of that. But the explosives were set. Ahsoka pushed the button on the detonator and the shield was destroyed. The Republic was now able to destroy the droid army!

The battle was over. The Republic had won! Finally, after returning to camp, Anakin and Ahsoka reported back to Yoda. He asked how Ahsoka was doing. *Uh-oh*, thought Ahsoka as she turned to Anakin.

"I admit that Ahsoka is a little rough around the edges," Anakin said. That didn't sound good. ". . . But with training, she might be able to amount to something." Anakin smiled down at Ahsoka. She had done well after all.

"Then go with you she will, to the Teth

system," Yoda said. Rotta, Jabba the Hutt's son, had been kidnapped. The Jedi and his student were off to Teth to help find him.

It was time for Ahsoka's first real mission and she was excited! She had been training to become a Jedi for a very long time. Now she was boarding a spaceship, ready for adventure!

Before she left, though, Yoda warned it would be hard. She should have listened to him; it would turn out to be more dangerous than Ahsoka ever could have dreamed.

CHAPTER 2

Anakin and Ahsoka's gunship dropped out of space. A hundred other spaceships flew with them. The battle had already begun. Ships exploded all around.

"This isn't practice, Ahsoka," Anakin yelled over the noise. R2-D2 blipped, agreeing.

Hmph, Ahsoka thought. "I know, and I'll try not to get you killed," she joked. But she was desperate to prove herself to her Master.

BOOM! A blast hit their ship! Ahsoka looked

out the window. Their wing engine was smoking! Down below, Ahsoka saw a temple on top of a hill. It was their only shot.

Anakin and Ahsoka jumped out at the last minute, R2-D2 right behind them. Their ship exploded seconds later. Hundreds of clone troopers dropped right behind them into the jungle of Teth. Droids started firing from everywhere. Anakin yelled at the troops to follow him. Up ahead was a temple, hidden in the trees. The little Huttlet, Rotta, was in there, somewhere.

"Here we go," Ahsoka said to herself. She was scared. Yoda said that fear is a way to the dark side of the Force. So Ahsoka tried to calm herself down. But as she rushed up toward the droids, it was hard not to be frightened.

Finally, Anakin and his Padawan made it to the top of the hill. Ahsoka slashed through a group of droids. The troopers held back the

rest as the Jedi and R2-D2 ran down into the
temple. Ahsoka looked up at Anakin, hoping
he saw how brave she was. But he wasn't even
paying attention.

That's when Ahsoka noticed it, too. "Master,
you know you're walking us into a trap," she
said. Ahsoka saw Separatist droids hiding in the
shadows. Ahsoka could also sense the dark side.
This wasn't good at all.

"I know," Anakin said. They snuck through
to the back of the temple. Just before they

opened the last door, a bunch of droids leaped out. Ahsoka quickly destroyed all of them. Well, almost. Anakin had to take out the last one. He wasn't happy that Ahsoka had missed it, but he didn't say much. He just opened the last temple door.

There sat Rotta, crying at the back of the dungeon. He wasn't as ugly as his father, Jabba. He did smell, though. *Yuck*, Ahsoka thought. She picked up the Huttlet and put him in her backpack. Rotta coughed, then gurgled. The young Jedi could feel his fever. This wasn't good!

"Master! We've got to find a way out of here," Ahsoka said. Rotta was definitely sick. He needed a doctor. "We can't let the little guy die!"

"Our job is to protect this Hutt. It's too dangerous," Anakin said. "You have to listen to me." Ahsoka grimaced. She *knew* he was going to say that.

"I do listen to you, Master. I just don't like being treated like I'm a youngling," Ahsoka said.

"You must have patience. What are you trying to prove anyway?" Anakin asked.

"That I'm not too young to be your Padawan," Ahsoka whispered. Anakin put his hand on her shoulder and smiled. Then his smile slowly disappeared. Ahsoka frowned. Something was off. They could sense it in the Force.

"Ventress!" Anakin said.

The Sith assassin? Ahsoka thought. *Was she why I could sense the dark side?*

"She's here to kill the Hutt," Anakin yelled.

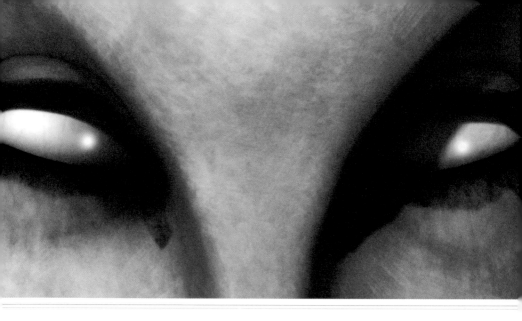

"Come on!" Anakin started to run. Ahsoka, with Rotta on her back, tried to keep up.

But it was too late. When they reached the stairs, four super battle droids blocked the exit. A cloaked figure stepped out. It dropped its cloak and lit two red lightsabers. It was Asajj Ventress, and she wasn't going to let the two Jedi go without a fight.

CHAPTER 3

"Master Skywalker," Ventress said, mocking the Jedi. The dark side flowed all around her. "I see you've found yourself a new pet!"

"I'm no pet," Ahsoka said. *I'm going to teach this Sith a lesson,* she thought. R2-D2 had other ideas, though. He plugged in to a computer and opened up the floor beneath Ventress and the droids. Unfortunately, Anakin and Ahsoka were standing in the same spot.

They all dropped down into a gloomy chamber.

As soon as they hit the bottom, though, Anakin and Ahsoka jumped into action. The droids were easy, but Ventress was impossible! The Jedi's lightsabers whirled in the dark, dank pit. With a swoop, Ventress almost got Ahsoka, but Anakin saved his Padawan at the last minute.

"I'll handle her," Anakin said. "Get the Huttlet out of here!"

Ahsoka wasn't going to let Anakin down again. He and Ventress fought as the young Padawan headed to the door with Rotta and R2-D2. Ahsoka smashed the controls on the wall. The door opened.

Ahsoka rushed outside and onto the landing platform. She was worried about Anakin, Ventress, and especially Rotta. The medics *had* to help him.

"Ahsoka, wait!" Anakin said. Suddenly, a shadow fell over his Padawan.

A vulture droid appeared out of nowhere. It bombed the platform. When Ahsoka looked up, she and Anakin were separated. The vulture droid had landed between them.

CHAPTER 4

Nothing was going right: Ventress, the vulture droid . . . Ahsoka blamed herself for it all. Maybe she wasn't ready to be a Jedi after all.

It didn't matter if Ahsoka was ready or not, though. The vulture droid was too busy shooting at her and Anakin. R2-D2 got knocked off of the platform and fell into the jungle as Rotta wailed.

"I wish you were home, too," Anakin said to Rotta, who was now being carried by the Jedi.

Suddenly, Ahsoka got a lucky slice in on the

vulture droid. Her lightsaber cut through its wing like butter. The droid howled and swung its other leg. It knocked her to the edge of the platform. She screamed, dangling helplessly over the edge.

The Jedi were in trouble, all right. Anakin couldn't get ahold of the clone troopers on his communication device. Ahsoka was about to get squashed by the vulture droid. Even R2-D2 was in danger. But Anakin wasn't going to leave his Padawan hanging there.

With a yell, he attacked the vulture droid. Ahsoka's eyes went wide as she watched. Her

Master seemed to be invincible! In a minute, the droid lay in pieces on the ground.

"Good distraction, Snips," Anakin said. "Let me guess, you meant to do that?"

Snips? Ahsoka thought. *Is that his new nickname for me? Ech.* "Distraction? I cut his wing off!" Ahsoka said.

"Give Artoo a hand," Anakin said, ignoring her. "I'll see if we can get a transport." Anakin started fiddling with his communicator.

Ahsoka huffed, but helped R2-D2 onto the platform. Gigantic dragonflies from the jungle had been poking him, but she scared them away. R2-D2 beeped, thanking her. "You're welcome, Artoo," Ahsoka said. "At least *someone* here appreciates my help."

Anakin was too busy to respond. He couldn't get through to anybody. That was bad enough. But then twin red lightsabers began cutting through the door to the temple. Ventress was coming back! The Jedi were trapped.

Anakin and Ahsoka yelled orders at each other, but Rotta squealed. The Padawan looked to where the Huttlet was pointing. Off in the distance, a starship sat on another landing platform. But a mile of jungle lay between it and the Jedi.

"How are we going to make it?" Ahsoka said.

"Like this!" Anakin said, and he jumped off of the platform with Rotta on his back. Ahsoka's mouth dropped. But before she could do anything, the doors flung open.

Ventress stormed out, eyes flaming. "Where is Skywalker?" she snarled. Ahsoka couldn't answer. Her lips were trembling.

"Here!" Anakin yelled as he flew in on one of the dragonflies. Ventress was too surprised to do anything. So Ahsoka jumped off of the platform before the assassin could get them. In a flash, Anakin had grabbed Ahsoka, and the dragonfly

soared off with R2-D2 jetting along beside them.
Rotta burped in Ahsoka's face just as she settled
in for the flight.

"I missed you, too," Ahsoka said. And
the strange thing was, she kind of did. Rotta
depended on her. So did the entire Republic.

The dragonfly flew toward the starship, and
Ahsoka tried to keep her grip.

CHAPTER 5

It was a long way on the back of that dragonfly, but everybody made it in one piece. They weren't out of the jungle yet. The ship on the platform looked like it could barely fly. R2-D2 bleeped, worried.

"We'd be better off on that big bug," Ahsoka said. But they didn't have much of a choice.

Anakin ordered Ahsoka to start up the engines. He went to make sure everything was safe. What he didn't know was that the freighter wasn't empty. As Ahsoka opened the doors, several droids popped out and started firing.

Ahsoka had learned a lot, however, just by watching her Master. With a few chops of her lightsaber, their circuits were sparking all over the ground. She rushed into the ship, with Anakin and R2-D2 right behind her.

"Now let's get this thing started up," Anakin said. He sat down in the pilot's seat and turned on the engine. Or, he tried to. Ahsoka sighed. *Great. What more could go wrong?*

"Relax, Snips," Anakin said.

He and R2-D2 went to work. Ahsoka tried

to keep Rotta from getting any sicker. He wasn't looking good at all. Soon, though, the ship roared to life and blasted off.

As the ship tore into the sky, Ahsoka turned to Anakin. "Master, today I did my best to stay calm and focused," she said. Anakin didn't say anything, but he smiled a bit. "When I did, everything seemed so easy." Anakin was about to say something, when . . . *CRACK!* A blast hit the ship.

"Well, things just got a lot harder," Anakin said. Tons of Separatist ships were closing in on the Jedi. Ahsoka huffed. She had been so close to getting her Master to open up.

Anakin had to focus on flying, and wow, was he good! He did loops, spins, and anything he could think of to get them out of range of the Separatists. *If I could ever be half as good as him,* Ahsoka thought, *that would be enough for me.*

But the ship was still too heavy to escape. The Jedi had to make it to Jabba's home on Tatooine.

Luckily, Anakin's Padawan had an idea and ran off down a hallway in the ship. "Ahsoka, wait!" Anakin shouted. But she was already gone.

Ahsoka rushed back into the cargo bay. Just like she thought! Junk and boxes crowded the entire room. Ahsoka opened up the bay doors as Anakin rolled the ship. Everything in there flew out. Ahsoka watched as it all smashed into the ships behind them. Problem solved!

Ahsoka rushed back up to the cockpit and

told Anakin about what she did. "You could have just opened the doors from here," Anakin said, pointing to the control panel. Ahsoka shrugged, then changed the subject.

"You grew up on Tatooine, right?" Ahsoka said, trying to get him to talk. "So, for you, this trip is like going home."

"Yeah. Home," Anakin repeated. His eyes glazed over. He was lost in thought. What about

Tatooine? Ahsoka wasn't going to get anything out of him. She sighed and searched for some medical supplies to help Rotta. Ahsoka began to worry that she was never going to please her Master.

The ship jumped into hyperspace. The Jedi were safe. For a little bit. Who knew what was waiting for them on Tatooine?

CHAPTER 6

"How's Stinky?" Anakin asked as they came
out of hyperspace. Ahsoka had found some
medical supplies and Rotta happily slept on
the floor.

"He seems to be doing much better," Ahsoka
said. "Even *you* have to admit that he's cute
when he's asleep." She looked out the window
and saw Tatooine down below. "I bet it feels
great to be back," Ahsoka told him. Anakin
just grunted.

"I was hoping never to lay eyes on this dust ball again," Anakin said.

Wow. Underneath his skin, he wasn't so tough after all. "Okay, what happened?" Ahsoka asked.

"I don't want to talk about it," Anakin said. His Padawan almost said something, but didn't. Anakin smiled at her. They'd been through a lot. He was harsh sometimes, but Ahsoka knew he was just looking out for her.

There wasn't time for any apologies, though. Separatist ships appeared out of nowhere and attacked. Rotta woke up and started crying.

"Somebody doesn't want Stinky to get home in one piece," Anakin said. He turned on the shields, and they were in battle once again.

Anakin and Ahsoka's talk had to wait. They were so close to Tatooine, but the Separatists had found them even here. They must have known all along that the Jedi would come. But how?

Anakin wasn't thinking about that, though. He fought his way down to the planet below. R2-D2 took over the guns and blasted Separatists left and right. They made quite a team . . . except for Ahsoka. All she could do was watch. She felt scared and excited at the same time. It was almost fun!

But then a droid got in a lucky shot. *BAM!* The engines began to smoke as the freighter hurtled toward Tatooine's surface. Anakin tried the controls, but nothing worked.

"This is going to be a bumpy landing," Anakin yelled. Ahsoka held onto Rotta as the desert

raced up to meet them. In a few seconds, they would hit. And that wasn't going to be any fun at all.

CHAPTER 7

Ahsoka didn't remember when she woke up. One minute, it was pitch black in the spaceship. The next, Anakin pulled her out of the wreckage. The sun nearly blinded them both. Rotta seemed happy, though.

"Welcome home, Stinky," Ahsoka said.

Tatooine's endless desert stretched out ahead of them. They couldn't see anything but sand. And it was hot. *Very* hot. Ahsoka turned to her Master. He didn't look too happy, either.

"Jabba's palace is on the other side of the Dune Sea," Anakin said. It was a long way off, but Anakin grew up there and he knew where he was going. They set off to finish their mission.

Still, Anakin wasn't talking much. Ahsoka remembered a saying of Yoda's: "Old sins cast long shadows." She asked Anakin what it meant.

"He means your past can ruin your future if you allow it," he replied. "But Master Skywalker was the one who said, 'I don't want to talk about my past.'"

"Okay, fine," Ahsoka said. Anakin went quiet

again. Ahsoka pouted silently.

But then she stopped dead in her sandy tracks. Something wasn't right. Ahsoka could feel it under her skin. R2-D2 beeped, worried. "We're not alone," Ahsoka said.

"I sense it, too," Anakin said. "It's the dark side of the Force." That could only mean one thing . . .

Count Dooku was on Tatooine! And he would do anything to prevent the Jedi from saving Rotta. Ahsoka didn't think she was ready to handle a Sith Lord like Dooku, but she wanted to stay and fight with her Master. Anakin had other ideas.

"I need you to trust me on this one," Anakin said. He took Rotta out of his backpack. Then he began filling it with rocks. Ahsoka raised an eyebrow. She wasn't sure what her Master was doing, but helped anyway.

Then she got it! Master Anakin was going to trick Dooku. He'd send her ahead with Rotta. When the Count found him, Dooku would think that Anakin had the Hutt. It was dangerous, but Anakin wouldn't listen. He sent Ahsoka and R2-D2 away as Dooku appeared on the horizon.

Ahsoka looked back as she snuck away.
Dooku and Anakin lit up their lightsabers and
fought. It was amazing to see. But Ahsoka had
to hurry before Dooku realized what was up. So
she ran through the desert to Jabba's palace.

Ahsoka worried about Anakin, but not too
much. If anybody could handle Dooku, it was
her Master. He'd taught her so much already.
And now Anakin trusted her with Rotta. Ahsoka
hurried through the desert. She didn't want

to disappoint him.

Finally, Ahsoka reached the palace. As she walked up the path, it seemed like everything had turned out all right. But Ahsoka was thinking about Anakin and listening to the Force, and when Ahsoka reached the gates, three MagnaGuards jumped out of the sand. The powerful droids growled and reached out. Ahsoka whipped out her lightsaber. It was just her and R2-D2 against the droids. There was no backing down now.

CHAPTER 8

The MagnaGuards attacked, knocking
R2-D2 out of the way. Ahsoka didn't have time
to think. She just let her lightsaber fly in her
hands. The MagnaGuards stabbed and slashed,
but Ahsoka somehow danced away.

Suddenly Anakin appeared on top of a
landspeeder in the distance. He must have
beaten Count Dooku. But instead of stopping,
he just rocketed past Ahsoka. She knew that
she was hard to see, so she jumped up to get

his attention. She really needed help with the MagnaGuards!

"Master! Master!" Ahsoka yelled, but he didn't hear her. He just raced toward Jabba's palace. *He never listens,* Ahsoka fumed. She had to end her fight quickly! There was no telling what kind of trouble her Master would get into without her!

The three MagnaGuards pounced. One, two . . . *three*! Ahsoka slashed them with her lightsaber. They fell to the ground in pieces.

"Let's get you home, Rotta," Ahsoka said. Rotta gurgled as the Padawan lifted him onto her back. Ahsoka looked around and found R2-D2 beeping in the sand. "You too. Master Anakin needs us."

The three raced into the palace. Ahsoka almost got them all lost in the dark tunnels. Finally, she found her way to Jabba's throne room.

But Jabba was about to have Anakin killed. His cronies were all pointing their weapons at Ahsoka's Master. "Stop!" she yelled and everybody turned to look at her. Ahsoka gulped.

"Most patient Jabba," Ahsoka said. She tried to keep her voice from trembling. "Your son has arrived, alive and well."

"He *is* alive, isn't he?" Anakin whispered.

"And still stinky," Ahsoka said. *That* was for sure.

Jabba roared. His guards came down and snatched Rotta out of Ahsoka's hands. Rotta squealed when he saw his dad. Jabba hugged his son. It was almost cute. Almost.

But Jabba wasn't done with the Jedi. He yelled again. His guards pointed their guns back at them.

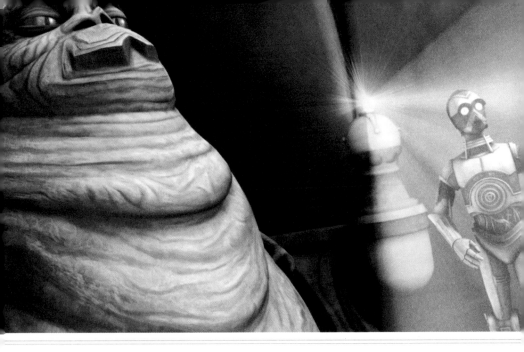

"Another fight?" Ahsoka said. "This is getting old!"

Just before they could shoot, though, a hologram activated. It was Padmé Amidala, the Galactic Senator! And she had a message for the Hutts.

"Greetings, honorable Jabba," Padmé said. "I am Senator Amidala of the Galactic Republic." She explained that Jabba's uncle had been the one who had stolen Rotta. Count Dooku had even helped.

Ahsoka's mind reeled. They'd been set up all along! The Separatists had lied to Jabba. They said the Jedi were the ones who'd kidnapped his son. Dooku had tried to kill Rotta so he could blame the Republic!

Anakin thanked the Senator. Then he turned to his Padawan. Ahsoka didn't know what he was going to say. But he didn't say anything. He just bowed. Ahsoka bowed back. She hid her smile. *I guess I did well after all*, she thought.

And with that, Ahsoka's first mission was a success. Everything turned out okay. Dooku was

defeated. Jabba got his son back. And Ahsoka
even impressed her teacher. Obi-Wan Kenobi
and Master Yoda flew down and congratulated
Anakin and Ahsoka on a job well done.

The war wasn't over, though. Anakin and
Ahsoka had many more missions ahead of them.
But with Anakin leading the way, Ahsoka felt
confident. What could go wrong?